THIS BOOK BELONGS TO

The Adventures of
Bella & Harry
Let's Visit Edinburgh!

Written By
Lisa Manzione

Illustrated By
Kristine Lucco

Bella & Harry, LLC

www.BellaAndHarry.com
email: BellaAndHarryGo@aol.com

Hi friends! Harry and I are so happy to see you. As you know, we love to travel with our family and we are about to depart for our next adventure. So come on, let's go!

5

Orkney
Islands

Outer Hebrides

North
Sea

Scotland

Atlantic
Ocean

☆ EDINBURGH

Northern
Ireland

England

"**Next** stop... Edinburgh, Scotland. We are off to see the Royal Edinburgh Military Tattoo!"

"The Military Tattoo, Bella? What is the Military Tattoo?"

"**Well** Harry, the Military Tattoo is a festival held at Edinburgh Castle. The performers are military musicians, mainly using bagpipes and drums during their show."

"**The** festival takes place in the month of August each year. It is a very exciting event full of music, marching and fun."

9

"**Harry**, did you know that Edinburgh Castle has been here for hundreds of years? The castle is built on Castle Rock, which was formed after a volcano millions of years ago."

"**Bella**, what is that small building near the big castle?"

12

"**Harry**, that building is St. Margaret's Chapel. The chapel is the oldest building in all of Edinburgh. The inside of the building is about ten feet wide, or about ten very cute Chihuahuas standing in a straight line!"

"Come on Harry! We are off to see more sights and sounds of Scotland

"**Look** Harry! Our children are getting dressed in their family plaid at one of the local shops. Family history is very important in Scotland. Each family has a crest and coat of arms, along with a plaid fabric or tartan, that represents their family history."

AVISE LA FIN

"Harry! Harry! What are you doing?"

"Come on Bella! Let's get dressed in our family plaid with the children! This is fun!"

"**You** are right Harry, that was fun, but it is time to go!
Before we leave, let's look at a map of Scotland."

"**Harry**, do you remember Scotland is part of Great Britain? We learned about Great Britain when we visited London, England."

"**Yes**, Bella, I remember all about Great Britain. Great Britain is different than the United States because we have a President, along with Congress. Great Britain has a King or Queen, and Parliament that help to run the country."

"Correct, Harry!"

"**Off** we go! We are now walking down the 'Royal Mile'. Harry, the 'Royal Mile' connects Edinburgh Castle to the Palace of Holyroodhouse or Holyrood Palace."

"**Holyrood** Palace is the official home of the Royal Family while they are visiting Scotland. It was built hundreds of years ago."

21

"**Time** to move on!
We are going to watch our
children practice falconry!"

"Falconry? What is falconry Bella?"

Falconry

22

"**Falconry** is the sport of hunting with falcons or hawks. Falconry has been around for thousands of years. You see Harry, the birds are trained to swoop down, catch their prey and bring it back to their owner!

Look out Harry, the birds hunt for live, small animals...about our size!!"

Swoosh... Swooshhhhh!!!!

"Bella! Bella!"

24

"**Ha! Ha!** Don't worry Harry, we are leaving now. We are off to see the countryside of Scotland and look for the 'Loch Ness Monster' or 'Nessie'!"

"Harry, the 'Loch Ness Monster' is just a story, but we will look for her anyway."

"**Bella**, I don't like monsters!"

"**Look** around Harry! We are in the Scottish Highlands.
Over there is Loch Ness where, it is said, 'Nessie' lives."

28

"**Bella**, what is a loch?"

"A loch is a lake. Loch Ness has more water in it than any other loch in Scotland. There is more water in this lake than there is in all of the lakes in England and Wales put together."

"**Harry**, the children are trying a Dundee cake. Dundee cakes are fruitcakes that taste good with a chunk of cheese and hot tea."

"Yummmy!"

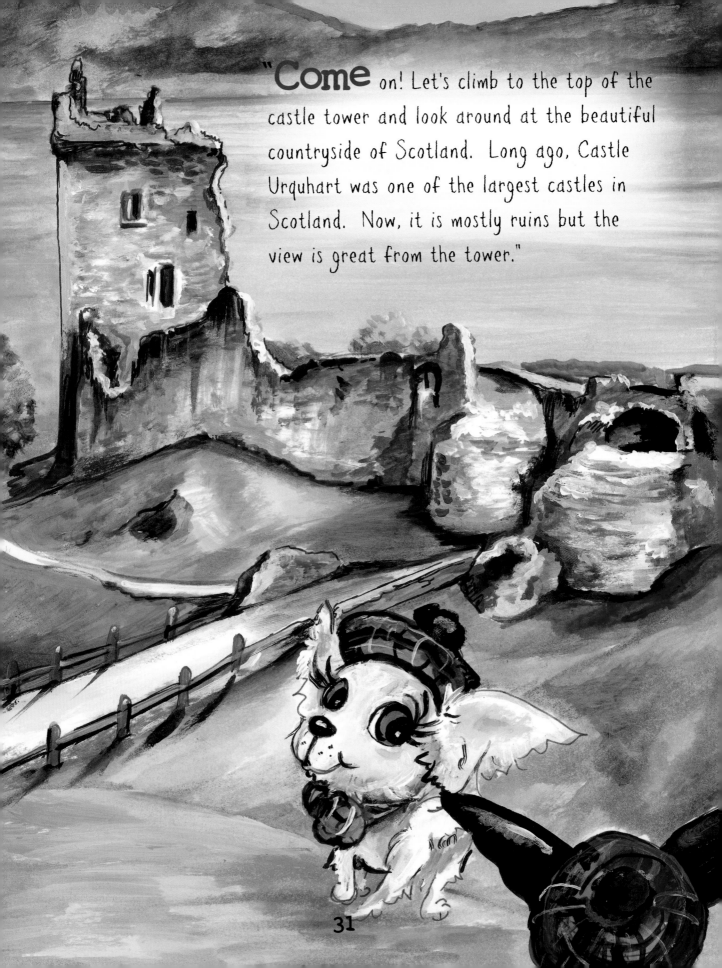

"**Come** on! Let's climb to the top of the castle tower and look around at the beautiful countryside of Scotland. Long ago, Castle Urquhart was one of the largest castles in Scotland. Now, it is mostly ruins but the view is great from the tower."

31

Well, Harry and I haven't seen "Nessie" but we are going to stay here at the Castle Urquhart to look for her. I know we will be leaving on another adventure very soon but for now, it's good-bye from... Bella Boo and Harry too!

Our Adventures in Scotland

Having fun with a Scottish Terrier!

Bella enjoying the beautiful Scottish countryside.

Bella and Harry visit the Royal Botanic Garden.

Bella and Harry visit Balmoral Castle.

Fun Scottish Words and Phrases

Yes – Aye

No – Nae

Family – Clan

Lake – Loch

Thank you – Thenk ye

You're welcome – Ye're welcome

Good morning – Guid morning

Good night – Guid nicht

Library of Congress Cataloging-in-Publications Data is available

Manzione, Lisa

The Adventures of Bella & Harry: Let's Visit Edinburgh!

ISBN: 978-1-937616-07-6

First Edition

Book Seven of Bella & Harry Series

For further information please visit:

www.BellaAndHarry.com

or

Email: BellaAndHarryGo@aol.com

CPSIA Section 103 (a) Compliant

www.beaconstar.com/ consumer

ID: L0118329. Tracking No.: MR29694-1-9641

Printed in China

Cairo
EDINBURGH
UK
EDINBURGH
Scotland
UK
EDINBURGH
FCB
VENICE
VENICE